My mom moved to a new hospital. She's an orthopedic surgeon. She can name and locate all 206 bones in the body from memory.

Mi mamá se cambió a un nuevo hospital. Ella es una cirujana ortopédica. Mi mamá puede nombrar y ubicar los 206 huesos del cuerpo de memoria.

My dad is an artist. Every year on my birthday he paints a portrait of me and Papá Yefferson.

Mi papá es un artista. Todos los años para mi cumpleaños pinta un retrato mío con Papá Yefferson.

YXEFFERSON, ACTUALLY

EN REALIDAD, ES YEFFERSON

Written by Katherine Trejo & Scott Martin-Rowe

Illustrated by Karla Monterrosa

Lil' LIBROS

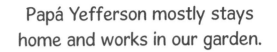

Papá Yefferson mostly stays home and works in our garden.

Papá Yefferson se queda principalmente en casa y trabaja en nuestro jardín.

I was named after him, which is so cool because he is my favorite person.

Me pusieron su nombre, lo cual es genial porque es mi persona favorita.

Good morning, everyone, and welcome! I want to introduce you to our new friend. This is Jefferson.
¡Buenos días a todos y bienvenidos! Quiero presentarles a nuestro nuevo amigo. Este es Jefferson.
Uh, it's actually...
Eeh, en realidad...
Let's welcome Jefferson to our school.
Démosle la bienvenida a Jefferson a nuestra escuela.

yeffe

I've never had to start over anywhere. I've had the same friends for as long as I can remember and we've always known the sounds and spellings of one another's names like they belonged to us.

RSON

Nunca he tenido que empezar de nuevo en ningún lado.
He tenido los mismos amigos desde que me acuerdo y
siempre hemos sabido los sonidos y la ortografía de los
nombres de los demás como si nos pertenecieran.

Nobody else got my name right for the rest of the day.

Nadie dijo mi nombre correctamente por el resto del día.

Hey Jefferson, want to play kickball with us?
¿Oye Jefferson, quieres jugar a la pelota con nosotros?
By the way, are you named after Thomas Jefferson or something?
Por cierto, ¿te llamas así en honor a Thomas Jefferson o qué?
No, I'm named after my grandpa.
No, me llamo así en honor a mi abuelo.
Is your grandpa named after Thomas Jefferson?
¿Tu abuelo se llama así en honor a Thomas Jefferson?
I don't think so.
No creo.
2

Your turn, Thomas Jefferson!
¡Tu turno, Thomas Jefferson!
That's not my name.
Ese no es mi nombre.

I had a lot of confusing feelings after school. Every night at dinnertime my family goes around and has to share one positive thing from their day. It seemed like everyone had a good day, and then it was my turn.

Tuve muchos sentimientos confusos después de la escuela. Todas las noches durante la cena, vamos uno por uno en mi familia compartiendo alguna cosa positiva de nuestro día. Parecía que todos tuvieron un buen día, y luego era mi turno.

I don't think anyone named Yefferson has ever gone to that school. Everyone got my name wrong today.
Creo que esta es la primera vez que alguien llamado Yefferson va a esa escuela. Hoy nadie dijo mi nombre correctamente.
What did you say when they said it wrong?
¿Qué les dijistes vos cuando lo dijeron mal?

Nothing.

Nada.

What would you have liked to tell them?

¿Qué te hubiera gustado decirles?

Well, I like how tall the Y stands compared to a J, and I like the sound the Y makes in Spanish, and mostly I like it because it's the same as Papá Yefferson and I wanna be like him when I grow up.

Bueno, a mí me gusta la altura de la Y en comparación con la J, y me gusta el sonido que hace la Y en español, y sobre todo me gusta porque tengo el mismo nombre que Papá Yefferson y quiero ser como él cuando sea grande.

So, what are you going to say tomorrow when they say your name wrong?

¿Y vos qué les vas a decir mañana cuando pronuncien mal tu nombre?

Good morning class, today we will learn about how plants make their own food through a process called photosynthesis. Has anyone here ever heard of photosynthesis?
Buenos días, hoy vamos a aprender cómo las plantas hacen su propio alimento a través de un proceso llamado fotosíntesis. ¿Hay alguien aquí que haya escuchado alguna vez sobre la fotosíntesis?
Yes, Jefferson?
¿Sí, Jefferson?

Hello Jefferson. Enjoy your lunch!
Hola Jefferson. ¡Que disfrutes tu almuerzo!
It's Yefferson, actually. And thank you, I love pepperoni pizza.
En realidad es Yefferson. Y gracias, me encanta la pizza de pepperoni.

You're up, Thomas Jefferson!
¡Te toca, Thomas Jefferson!
It's Yefferson, actually. And you better back up!
En realidad es Yefferson. ¡Y mejor empiecen a correr!

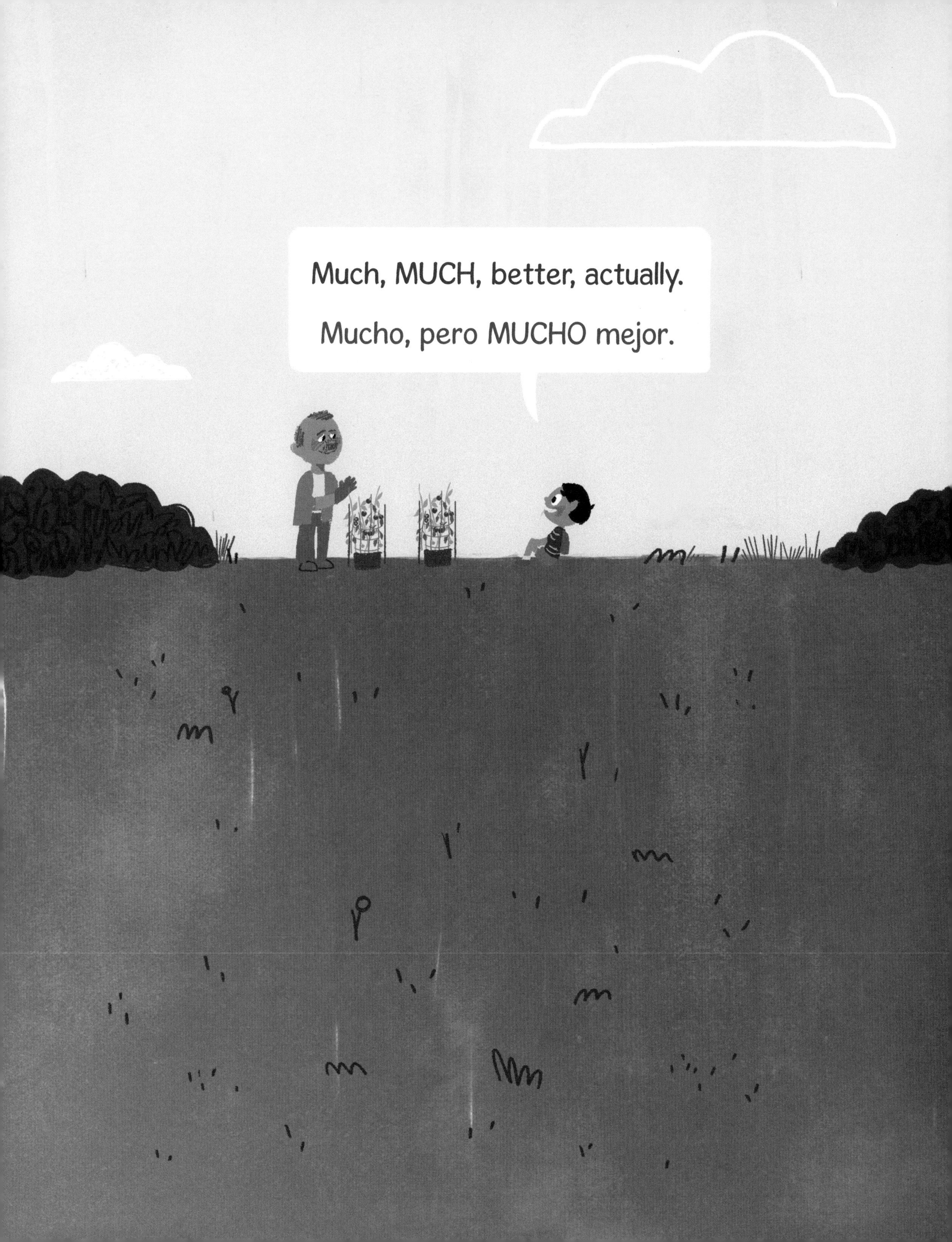
Much, MUCH, better, actually.
Mucho, pero MUCHO mejor.

Ahem, it's Yessica, actually.

Ejem, en realidad es Yessica.

Notes & Bios

Katherine

I want the children and adults who read this book to love and embrace their name, given or chosen, unapologetically. I hope this book serves as an avenue to self-advocacy for children, where something as small as reminding those around them to pronounce and spell their name affirms and empowers their identity. I hope this act of self-love and self-advocacy follows them into adulthood and inspires them to advocate for others. So, to all children, especially Black, Indigenous, and other children of color, may you always find the courage to stand up for yourself and be proud of your beautiful name.

Katherine Trejo is a first-generation Salvadoran-American college graduate with a bachelor's degree in Politics and Latin American/Latino Studies from UC Santa Cruz. She lives in Historic Filipinotown in Los Angles with her Boston Terrier Lily, mom, brother, cousins, aunts, grandma, niece, and nephew in the same apartment complex where she was raised. . She enjoys spending time with friends and family, watching cartoons, and listening to K-pop. She co-authored this book with Mr. Scott Martin-Rowe, one of her most influential and favorite teachers in high school.

Scott

For far too long, millions upon millions of children have gone into their school library or local bookstore and struggled to find someone on the cover who looks like them. I have always believed that it is through art and literature that we understand what it means to be human and to be connected to those around us. It's past time that we accept and love one another for who we are and everything that that means. Whether it be the language we speak, the foods we eat, the color of our skin, the name we are given, or anything else that makes us different, we must all see each other as a gift to the world and a treasure in one another's lives. I hope that this book is a small nudge in that direction.

Scott Martin-Rowe is a National Board Certified teacher-librarian in the Los Angeles Unified School District and the first in his family to graduate from college. Aside from teaching, he enjoys reading, writing, running, and spending time with his family and friends. He lives in Los Angeles with his wife, writer Kate Martin-Rowe, his four energetic children, one lazy dog, and an opinionated cat. Though he has many favorite students from his 15 years of teaching, Katherine Trejo is one of his most favorite (but don't tell the others).

Karla

I drew the children in this book inspired by kids I have seen around my neighborhood, my family, and old pictures of friends. I wanted to fill this book with kids who look like someone you might know because I think of each one of them as someone with a full life and a full story. While your life and family might look very different from Yefferson's, someone you know might have had a similar experience. I drew a world that is gentle, welcoming, and with room for everyone because I believe that world is possible and I hope seeing it illustrated helps you visualize it too.

Karla Monterrosa was born and raised in sunny San Salvador, El Salvador. She's an illustrator and animator on a mission to draw a world in which it's okay to feel awkward. Karla graduated from Emily Carr University of Art + Design with a BFA in Animation in 2013 and currently lives in the unceded, ancestral lands of the Musqueam, Squamish, and Thleil-Watuth nations, also known as Vancouver, BC.